MR. GRUMPY

by Roger Hargreaves

PSS!
PRICE STERN SLOAN

It was a lovely summer evening.

Mr. Grumpy was at home.

Crosspatch Cottage!

He sat down in an armchair, and picked up a book.

And then, do you know what he did?

He tore all the pages out of it!

Every one!

Mr. Grumpy can't stand books.

He has a shocking bad temper.

In fact, he's quite the most bad-tempered person you can imagine.

Grumpy by name, and even more grumpy by nature!

The following morning, he was out in his garden pulling up flowers (he couldn't stand pretty flowers growing in his garden), when out of the corner of his eye he saw a figure.

It was Mr. Happy.

"Good morning," said Mr. Happy.

"Good?" said Mr. Grumpy. "What's good about it?"

"But…," said Mr. Happy.

"But nothing," Mr. Grumpy went on. "Get out of my garden!"

"I beg your pardon?" said Mr. Happy.

"You heard me," snapped Mr. Grumpy. "Go away!"

"I say," laughed Mr. Happy. "You are a bad-tempered fellow!"

"Hmph!" grunted Mr. Grumpy.

"And," Mr. Happy went on, "bad-tempered fellows need to change their ways."

"Rubbish!" retorted Mr. Grumpy and went into his cottage, deliberately stepping on Mr. Happy's foot as he passed him.

"Ouch!" said Mr. Happy.

BANG! went the door of Crosspatch Cottage as Mr. Grumpy slammed it behind him.

Mr. Happy stood there, looking not quite so happy as he normally does.

His foot hurt!

He thought.

And thought.

And thought some more.

Then, he had an idea.

He smiled, and went to see Mr. Tickle.

Mr. Happy told Mr. Tickle of his idea of how to get Mr. Grumpy to change his ways, and Mr. Tickle grinned the sort of grin that goes from ear to ear.

That is, if you have ears, which he doesn't.

"Oh," he grinned, rubbing the hands at the end of those extraordinarily long arms of his together. "That sounds like fun!"

That afternoon, Mr. Grumpy went to town, shopping.

He walked into Mr. Meat's shop.

Mr. Meat was a butcher.

"Give me some sausages," snapped Mr. Grumpy. "And be quick about it!"

Poor Mr. Meat, who was frightened of Mr. Grumpy, did as he was told.

But, as he was doing as he was told, something appeared through his shop doorway.

Do you know what it was?

It was an extraordinarily long arm belonging to…

Well, you can guess who it belonged to.

Can't you?

That extraordinarily long arm of Mr. Tickle's came in through the door, and across the shop, and up to Mr. Grumpy, and tickled him.

"Oh!" squeaked Mr. Grumpy in alarm, dropping his sausages, and looking around to see what had happened.

But, could he see anything?

He could not!

"Hmph!" grunted Mr. Grumpy, and picked up his sausages, and went next door.

To the bakery.

CRASH! went the door of the shop.

"Give me a cake," snapped Mr. Grumpy. "And hurry up!"

Poor Mrs. Fairy, who sold cakes at the bakery, was frightened of Mr. Grumpy, so did as she was told.

But, as she was doing as she was told, guess what happened?

"Oh!" squeaked Mr. Grumpy, dropping his cake, and his sausages.

He just could not understand what was happening.

And, the same thing happened at Mr. Daily's (the newspaper stand), and at Mrs. Humbug's (the candy store), and at Mr. Bottle's dairy, and at Mr. Packet's (the grocer's).

It went on all afternoon!

And all afternoon, Mr. Grumpy kept being tickled, and dropping his shopping bags, and picking them up, and being tickled, and dropping his shopping bags, and picking them up, and being tickled, and dropping his shopping bags, and…

He just could not understand it.

On his way home to Crosspatch Cottage, he met Mr. Happy again.

"Hello," grinned Mr. Happy. "Having a nice day?"

"Get out of my way," snapped Mr. Grumpy, "before I kick you!"

But, almost before the words had passed his lips, that extraordinarily long arm of Mr. Tickle's had appeared from behind a tree and tickled him yet again.

He jumped in the air, and dropped all his shopping bags (yet again), and fell over.

Mr. Happy looked down at Mr. Grumpy lying amid a jumble of sausages and cake and newspapers and candy and milk and cornflakes.

"I think," he laughed, "that if you were to change your ways and be not quite so bad-tempered quite so often, this sort of thing might not happen to you quite so often."

"Hmph!" grunted Mr. Grumpy.

He picked up all his shopping bags (yet again) and went home to Crosspatch Cottage.

But on his way he did think about what Mr. Happy had said, because he very definitely did not like what had happened to him that afternoon.

Mr. Happy and Mr. Tickle laughed and shook hands.

And so, after that, he did try to be not quite so bad-tempered quite so often.

And, the more he tried the less he found he was tickled, and so he tried more and more, and these days he's a changed person.

Why, only the other evening, he picked up a book, and do you know what?

He only tore out one page!